War and Peace

Illustrated by Toni Goffe

Child's Play (International) Ltd
Swindon   **Bologna**   **New York**
© M. Twinn 1991   ISBN 0-85953-356-5 (soft cover)   Printed in Singapore
ISBN 0-85953-366-2 (hard cover)

There is usually no need to quarrel and fight.

So, why do we, sometimes?

Perhaps, we want something we can't have.
Or we disagree about something.
Or we don't trust someone.
Or we just get out of bed on the wrong side.

It may be somebody else's fault. They started it.

We will probably think so, or say so, anyway.

There are families, who almost never disagree.
If they do, they discuss calmly.
They listen to each other's point of view.
They try to understand.

In the end, they reach a decision,
which pleases everyone.

They don't fall out.
And if they do, they quickly make up.

Because they respect and love each other.

But even families,
who argue all the time,
usually stand together...

... when the family is threatened.

It is the same
with groups of people.

People, who work together or play together
or share common interests or opinions,
unite against rival groups.

But when a bigger cause comes along,
they unite with their rivals
against the common foe.

WORLD · CUP

It is the same story with political parties and with nations.

People rally to support their leaders.

Just as each of us thinks that he or she is right, families, groups, politicians and nations think that they are right.

When nations quarrel,
we stand united behind our flag,
our uniform, our beliefs, history,
traditions and culture.

And behind our fighting men and women.

If we could see the other side,
they feel and behave in the same way.

They are just like us.

If we only listened
to the other side's point of view,
we could often resolve problems
and arguments without fighting.

If we act in the heat of the moment,
it is soon too late to avoid conflict.

Injury piles upon injury,
insult on insult, lie on lie.

Hatred of the foe
and pride in ourselves
fan the flames.

Throughout history, nations have gone to war to acquire possessions, land and slaves.

Some became strong. They built great empires. Victory justified their actions.

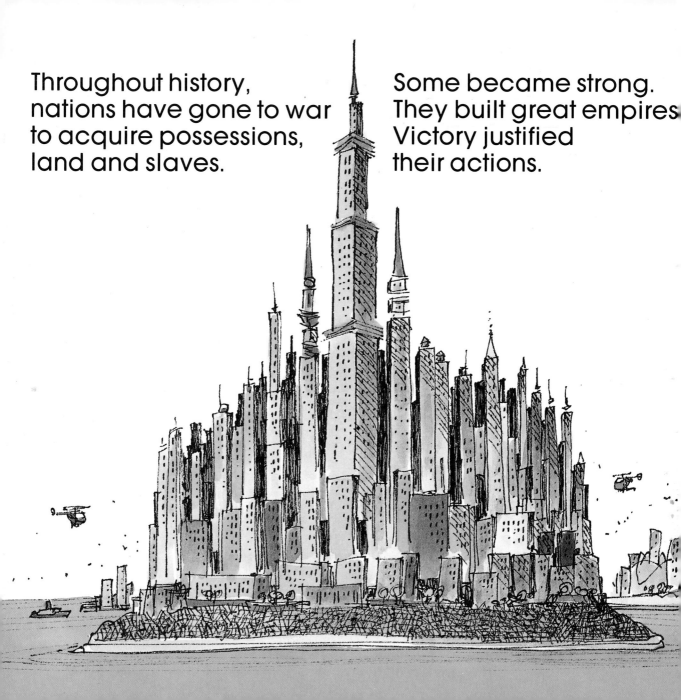

Entire races were wiped out.

And this has gone on
right down to the present day.

Today, weapons are so devastating,
that war doesn't make sense.

Nobody can win.

Soldiers no longer see
those they kill or maim
at the push of a button.

Wars destroy the progress of past generations, bringing their toil and aspirations to nothing.

Isn't it CRAZY?

Nothing makes a nation sadder than defeat.

But, even after victory, we sometimes
have to accept bitter truths.

Looking back, it is easy to see
who was right and who was wrong.

We know our country made mistakes,
especially when wars were fought far from home.
Years later, we still feel sad, angry, bitter and guilty.

So, why do we make the same mistakes?
Why do we go to war so readily?
Why do we supply arms
to dangerous leaders?

Why don't we ask questions at the right time?

And yet, as long as there is a danger,
each nation has to be prepared.
Each of us may have to answer the call.

That's the craziest part!

We should have learned by now,
that all people have a right to live
the way they want, as long as
they do not threaten the rights of others.

It is easy to judge other people's problems.
But when it is our nation's turn to listen, will we?

It may take centuries for nations to learn
to resolve disputes peacefully.

There may need to be a world government,
with sufficient military strength at its command.

Powerful nations may cede control of weapons.

Weaker nations may agree not to arm.

A peace-keeping force will keep enemies apart.

It is hard to imagine a world without war.

There are three ways in which nations may cease to fight each other.

One is, united against a common foe, like an enemy from space.

Another is less likely:
a change in human nature,
when people lose the taste for fighting.

The third is unthinkable:
when we have destroyed each other.

Wars produce supreme examples
of human sacrifice and heroism.

But how many are prepared to be branded
a coward for refusing to fight?

Who, when fighting in a just cause,
will pray for forgiveness
instead of victory?

Who will forgive the enemy?

Who has the courage
to question the leaders?

It is easier to make war than peace.

In a peaceful world,
when all nations and people live together
as friends, neighbours and family,
we can still be heroes …

...and enjoy triumphant victories over hunger, poverty and disease.

But we can't wait for nations,
groups or families to see sense.

It has to start with each one of us.

There are more of us than we think.
We can convince the others.

Let's do something about it. NOW!
Let's live in peace.
Let's share our world.